Earthstar Magic

by RUTH CHEW

Illustrated by the author

HASTINGS HOUSE · PUBLISHERS

New York, N.Y. 10016

LIBRARY OF CONGRESS CATALOGING IN PUBLICATION DATA

Chew, Ruth.
    Earthstar magic.

    SUMMARY: Ellen and Ben meet a friendly witch who
reveals the magic power of the earthstar to them.
    [1. Magic—Fiction. 2. Witches—Fiction] I. Title.
PZ7.C429Ear 1979   [Fic]   79-17927
ISBN 0-8038-1955-2

Published simultaneously in Canada by Saunders of To-
ronto, Ltd., Don Mills, Ontario

Printed in the United States of America

To my mother,
Pauline L. Chew

1

"Ellen," Ben whispered, "listen!"

Ben Sanders and his sister were lying on their stomachs on an old hunters' platform. It was built high in an old pine tree.

Ellen heard a rustling noise. She looked over the edge of the platform.

Somebody was crawling around in the woods below. It was a woman in a green sweater and a long brown skirt. She seemed to be looking for something in the dry leaves on the ground.

"Oh dear, oh dear, why did I have to drop it?" Ben and Ellen heard her say.

The woman bent over so far, Ellen thought her nose must be on the ground. Suddenly Ellen saw her reach out and grab something. The woman dropped it into a small plastic bag. Then she jumped to her feet.

Now Ben and Ellen could see that she was tall and skinny, and her hair was gray.

The woman peeked into the plastic bag. She gave it a little pat and skipped up the path and over the top of the hill.

Ellen was surprised to see her move so fast.

"There's something funny about her," Ben said. "I wonder what she has in that bag."

"Let's see what she's up to." Ellen backed off the platform until her feet touched a board that was nailed to the tree. All the way down to the ground there were boards to use as steps. Ellen climbed down the tree.

Ben came after her. He was two years younger than Ellen. Last year his legs weren't long enough to reach from one board to the next. It was still hard for him to climb down from the platform.

A narrow path led up the hill from the

foot of the tree. Ben and Ellen started up the path. They tried not to make any noise.

It was dark and shadowy in the woods. Here and there a shaft of sunlight sifted down through the tall trees. A chipmunk squeaked and ran under a stone. High overhead a woodpecker was tapping on the trunk of a tree.

At the top of the hill, Ellen looked down the other side. It was like an open meadow that went down to the big lake far below. The ground was rough and covered with weeds. Ellen saw the woman in the green sweater and brown skirt halfway down the hill. "Look, Ben. There she is."

Ben was pulling a raspberry off a bush that grew just at the edge of the woods. "Try one of these."

Ellen tasted a berry. "They're not ripe yet." She turned to look at the woman again.

There was no one on the hill.

"That's funny," Ellen said. "She was right over there a moment ago."

"Maybe she's hidden by the bushes." Ben stepped out of the woods.

Ellen ran down the slope and jumped over a tiny stream. "Watch your step, Ben."

Ben had already stepped into a marsh. His sneakers were all wet. "I never knew there was so much water here."

The two children walked through patches of daisies and around clumps of purple bee balm. On the other side of some cattails they came to a pile of rocks.

"Look, Ben," Ellen said, "there's a little pool here."

Plop! A green frog jumped from a rock into the pool.

Ben bent down to look into the water. "I can't see him. He must be hiding."

Ellen got down on her hands and knees at the edge of the pool. She brushed against something that was lying on a rock.

It was a small plastic bag.

2

"Why do people have to leave trash around?" Ellen stuffed the plastic bag into the pocket of her jeans. She could throw it away when she got home.

Ben was still looking for the frog. "See if you can find a stick, Ellen. I want to poke under these rocks."

"You might hurt the frog." Ellen leaned over the pool. "Look at those little jelly lumps. Do you think they're frog's eggs, Ben?"

Ben had an idea. "Hey, maybe that was the mother frog! There she is!"

Ellen stared into the pool. "Where?"

The frog was peeking out of a little underwater cave. Ben reached into the pool and made a sudden grab. "Got her!"

The frog wiggled, but Ben held her
fast.

"You're scaring her, Ben," Ellen said.
"Put her back into the water."

The frog stopped wiggling and looked
at Ben with her big eyes. He set her
down on a stone at the edge of the pool.
The frog sat there without moving.

"There's something wrong with her,"
Ben said. "Why doesn't she jump back
into the water?"

Ellen looked hard at the frog. "Maybe you squeezed her too tight."

"I didn't squeeze her at all," Ben said. "I just held onto her."

Ellen heard a faraway sound. "Listen!"

Now Ben heard it too.

Bong! Bong! Bong!

Ellen got to her feet. "We'd better go home. Let's take the shortcut over the cliff."

"What about the frog? If she stays out in the open a bird will eat her. There's a kingfisher that hangs around the cliff. I'm going to take her with me." Ben picked up the frog. "The eggs don't need the frog to sit on them."

Bong! Bong! Bong!

Ellen ran across the hillside. Ben followed her. They went up an old truck trail that curved around another hill. Clumps of small trees hid them from the road and the parking lot by the lake below.

Ellen reached out to touch the fuzzy red fruit of a sumac tree.

Bong! Bong! Bong!

"Hurry!" Ben started to climb the steep hill. Ellen came up after him. They dived into the woods on the other side of the hill. A path went straight down. Ben and Ellen skidded down it. At the bottom of the hill they came out of the woods onto a dirt road.

They raced along till they reached a row of cottages. Their mother was standing on the road near cottage number eight. Mrs. Sanders was banging a big gong. Bong! Bong! Bong!

She looked at Ben and Ellen. "What took you so long?"

3

"Ben," Mrs. Sanders said, "you know I don't let you keep wild things as pets. It isn't fair to them. They belong outdoors."

Ben was quiet. He looked down at the little green frog he was holding. The frog looked back at him with big sad eyes.

Ellen followed her mother down the steps from the road and along the path to the cottage. "The frog is hurt, Mother. We want to take care of her until she's better."

Mrs. Sanders crossed the wooden runway to the porch. Ben came running down the path. He caught up to his mother. "What can we feed the frog, Mom?"

Mrs. Sanders stopped and took another look at the frog. "Maybe they sell fishfood in the supermarket in Hawley," she said. "Your frog would probably eat that."

Mr. Sanders was stretched out on a deck chair on the porch. He looked up. "Better put that frog in a pail with some water, Ben. And give it a stone to sit on."

"Be quick about it. Supper's almost ready." Mrs. Sanders hung the gong on the knob of the screen door. She went into the cottage.

Ben made a little home for the frog in the scrub pail beside the kitchen sink. Then they all sat down at the big table.

The Sanders family had driven to the cottage from Brooklyn in the morning.

Most of the day had been spent unpacking the car.

When supper was over, Mr. and Mrs. Sanders walked down to the dock. Mr. Sanders wanted to check over the motorboat. Both the boat and the canoe had been stored in a boat house since last summer.

Ellen and Ben stayed in the cottage. Tonight was Ellen's turn to wash the dishes. Ben dried them.

"I saved a piece of meat loaf for the frog." Ellen pulled it out of the pocket of her jeans. She put it on the stone in the pail beside the frog. The frog looked at the meat, but didn't eat it.

Ellen felt something else in her pocket. She took it out.

"What do you have there?" Ben asked.

"Trash," Ellen said. "Don't you remember I found it by the pool in the rocks?"

Ben took a good look at the plastic

bag. "Ellen," he said, "the woman in the woods was carrying a bag like that."

"There's something in it." Ellen opened the bag. She took out a little gray-brown thing that looked like a crocus bulb.

"Let me see it." Ben reached for the little bulb. It fell out of Ellen's hand into the pail with the frog.

The frog made a dive for it. But Ben snatched it away. "You can't eat this, you silly frog. Eat your meat loaf."

The frog gave a low croak.

Ben was holding the curly little bulb on the palm of his hand. "Look, Ellen!"

Ellen stared. Very slowly the bulb was opening. It spread out six brown points like a star. In the center of the star was a small white puff-ball.

4

"It's magic!" Ben whispered.

"I've seen a picture of something like this," Ellen said. "It was in a book."

Ben had been thinking. "Ellen," he said, "we never did find out where that woman went. She just disappeared. You know what I think?"

Ellen was still looking at the brown star with the puff-ball in the middle. "What do you think, Ben?"

"The woman in the woods was a witch," Ben said in a low voice.

Ellen laughed. "Don't be silly, Ben. She was just an old lady picking mushrooms. That's what this thing is. I remember now where I saw the picture. It was in Mother's mushroom book. Come on. I'll show you."

Ben put the little brown star on the drainboard by the sink. He followed Ellen into their parents' bedroom.

There was a stack of books on the dresser. Ellen picked up the bird guide. Under it was a book about wildflowers. Next there was one on trees in America. At the very bottom of the pile was a book as thick as a Brooklyn telephone book.

"One Thousand American Fungi," Ellen read.

Ben looked over Ellen's shoulder. She started to leaf through the book. Suddenly they heard the screen door bang.

"Mom and Dad must have come back," Ben said.

"Mother," Ellen called, "can you help us find something in your mushroom book?"

There was no answer.

"Please," Ellen said.

Still no answer.

Ellen and Ben went out of the bed-room into the big living-dining room. No one was there. But they were both sure they had heard someone open and close the screen door. The children looked around.

"That's funny." Ellen put the mush-room book on the big table. She went to look out of the kitchen window. It was getting dark outside. But Ellen could see someone skipping up the steps to the road.

It was a woman in a green sweater and a long brown skirt.

5

"Look, Ben." Ellen stared through the window into the darkness.

Ben ran to the window and looked out. The woman was at the top of the steps now. She walked quickly away up the dirt road.

"That's the woman we saw in the woods," Ellen said. "What's she doing here?"

"I told you she was a witch," Ben said. "She came back to get the magic mushroom."

Ellen looked at the drainboard. "It's gone. Maybe it rolled onto the floor." She bent down to look for it.

The screen door opened. Mr. and Mrs. Sanders came into the cottage.

"What are you looking for?" Mr.

Sanders asked. "Did your frog get loose?"

"She's right here," Ben said. He looked into the pail. "No she isn't!"

"Look behind the stone," his father said.

But the frog wasn't there.

Ellen had been thinking. "The frog must have jumped onto the drainboard to eat the mushroom," she said.

The whole family searched the cottage. Mrs. Sanders looked on the kitchen shelves and on top of all the dressers. Ellen looked under the two sofas in the living-dining room. She used her little red flashlight to see under the beds.

Ben checked behind the hot water heater in the kitchen and in back of the

toilet in the bathroom. Mr. Sanders shook all the shoes and slippers that were on the floor. And everybody looked in the shower.

There wasn't a sign of the frog anywhere.

"I told you wild things like to be outdoors," Mrs. Sanders said. "The frog went back where it belongs."

"Ellen," Ben whispered, "you know what I think?"

"What?" Ellen asked him.

"The witch came back for her mushroom. And she took the frog too," Ben said.

Mrs. Sanders picked up the big book from the dining table. "What were you doing with my mushroom book?"

"I was trying to find a picture of a mushroom we saw today," Ellen said.

Mrs. Sanders handed her the book. "It's nearly bedtime. But you can look for the mushroom while Ben takes his shower."

When Ben had finished his shower and was all ready for bed, Ellen showed him two drawings in the book. They were on page 580. One was a side view of the puff-ball standing up on the points of the star.

"Spooky," Ben said. "It looks like an octopus."

The other drawing showed it all curled up like a crocus bulb.

"That's just the way we first saw it," Ben said. "It's the same mushroom all right."

"It's called an earthstar," Ellen told him. "I tried to read about it. But the words were too hard."

Mrs. Sanders walked over and took the book. "Your turn for a shower, Ellen. Off to bed, Ben."

6

Ben woke Ellen very early in the morning. The birds were twittering outside. And it was just beginning to get light. Mr. and Mrs. Sanders were still asleep.

"Don't waste the day in bed," Ben whispered. "Come on down to the lake. Mom and Dad won't be up for hours."

Ellen slid out from under the covers. "Br-r-r! It's cold." She put on a shirt and jeans and pulled on a warm sweater. She saw that Ben was wearing his new rubber clogs.

"My sneakers are still wet," he said.

Ellen decided to wear clogs too.

They unhooked the screen door and went out onto the porch. Ellen was careful not to let the door bang behind them.

"Ben," she whispered. "The phoebes are back again this year."

Ben looked at the top of the pole in the corner of the porch. A fluffy brown bird was sitting on a nest there.

"I wonder how those frog's eggs are doing," Ben said.

The people in the other cottages seemed to like to sleep late. Ben and Ellen didn't see anybody on the dirt road. And there was no one on the tree-covered hill going down to the lake.

They walked down a path till they came to the narrow beach. The lake was covered with a thick white mist. Through the mist Ben and Ellen could see a man fishing from the dock next to theirs.

Ellen went over to a green canoe on the beach. It was lying upside down on two sawhorses.

"Where are the paddles, Ben?"

Ben ran out to the end of the dock

that belonged to cottage number eight. He looked into a motorboat that was tied to the dock. "Dad keeps them in the boat." Ben pulled two long paddles out from under the back seat. He found two orange life jackets tucked into a shelf in the side of the boat. "The Lake Patrol will stop us if we don't wear these."

Ben and Ellen strapped on the life jackets and put the canoe into the water. Ben climbed into the front of the canoe. Ellen got into the back so she could steer. She used her paddle to shove the canoe out into deep water.

The two children felt like Indians as they paddled through the mist. Trees hid the cottages. The parking lot was around a bend of the lake.

They paddled steadily for a while. The sun rose over the treetops. The mist broke up into little wisps and puffs and was gone. The lake sparkled.

Ben looked over the side of the canoe.

"There's a whopper of a fish down there. The big ones come out early in the morning. Why don't we head over to Shuman Point? I'll bet we'd see a lot of fish there."

Ellen turned the canoe and began to paddle toward a long point of land that stuck out into the lake. No cottages were built there. It was all woods.

Ben pointed to a place on the rocky shore. A deer with two short horns had come out of the woods there to drink from the lake. He raised his head and sniffed the air. Then he flapped his white tail and crashed back into the woods.

"That was a buck," Ben said. "I guess we scared him."

Ellen looked into the woods after the deer. The trees grew on a steep rocky slope. "Ben, I think I see a cave."

7

"A cave? Where?" Ben was so excited that he stood up in the canoe. It tipped to one side. He sat down and held onto both sides until the canoe stopped rocking.

"Take it easy!" Ellen said. She pointed to the top of the hill. "Can you see that dark place in the rocks up there?" She paddled close to the shore.

Ben tried to look through the trees.

"Let's go up there and see if there really is a cave."

When they were in shallow water, Ben and Ellen stepped out of the canoe. They carried it up onto the shore and hid it behind some rocks.

They left their life jackets in the canoe with the paddles and started up the rocky slope.

It was hard to climb in the rubber clogs. Their feet kept sliding out of the back of them. One of Ben's clogs rolled most of the way down the hill. He had to go after it.

"Let's go barefoot." Ellen jammed her clogs into the back pockets of her jeans.

Ben tucked his clogs under his belt.

"Watch out for poison ivy," Ellen said.

They zig-zagged up the hill, going from one rock to the next. The trees seemed to grow right out of the rocks.

When they were close to the top of the hill, they walked along a ridge. Ben saw a shadowy place under an overhanging rock. "Is that what you saw?"

Ellen nodded.

It was tricky climbing the rock. Ellen had to use both hands. She pulled herself up onto a ledge in front of the cave. Then she lay down on her stomach and grabbed Ben's hands to help him up.

They stepped into the cave. It was dark inside, but after a few minutes their eyes began to get used to it.

The cave was bigger than it looked from outside. Ellen and Ben walked through a tunnel that went back into the hill. It widened out into something like a room.

Ben grabbed Ellen's arm.

In the dim light they saw somebody lying near them on the floor of the cave. It looked like a woman.

"Do you think she's dead?" Ben said.

8

The woman stirred. She let out a snore.

"She's only asleep," Ellen whispered. "Let's get out of here."

The two children turned to run out of the cave. But they were too late. A bony hand grabbed hold of Ellen's ankle. "Who's there?" a raspy voice asked.

Ellen felt as if she were frozen. She couldn't move. She couldn't speak.

The woman sat up. She let go of Ellen's ankle and started to feel around in the dim light for something. The next minute she struck a match and lit a bit of candle that was stuck to the floor of the cave.

Now Ben and Ellen could see that she was wearing a green sweater and a brown skirt.

Ellen shivered. Her ankle still felt cold
from the touch of the woman's hand.
She looked at the woman's face. Her
nose was long and pointed. And so was
her chin. She brushed her scraggly gray
hair back and looked at Ellen with
bright green eyes.

Ellen's heart seemed to stop beating.

"Good morning," the woman said.
"You're up early."

She's pretending to be friendly, Ellen
thought. We'd better act as if we believe
her.

"We saw you in the woods yesterday," Ben said.

"Yes." The woman stood up and stretched. "You're Ben. And that's your sister, Ellen."

"How do you know our names?" Ben asked. "You must be a witch!"

Why did Ben always say such terrible things? Ellen wished she could shove the words back into his mouth. "Be careful, Ben!" she said in a low voice.

Ben stared at the woman. She was blinking her green eyes. And her face was starting to get red. The corners of her mouth began to turn down.

"Oh, Ellen, she's going to do something awful to us!" Ben tried to pull Ellen toward the mouth of the cave.

But Ellen didn't move. She was still looking at the woman's face.

Ben was frantic. "Run!" he said.

9

Ellen thought she saw something shiny on the woman's wrinkled cheek. A moment later a fat tear rolled down.

All of a sudden everything seemed different. Ellen wasn't afraid anymore.

"Stop it, Ben!" she said. "You've hurt her feelings." She yanked her hand away from Ben and gently touched the woman's arm. "Don't cry," Ellen said. "Ben didn't mean it. Of course you're not a witch."

The woman looked at Ellen with wet green eyes. "That's just the trouble."

"What do you mean?" Ellen asked.

The woman sniffed. She swallowed hard. "If you must know," she said in a very small voice, "they took my hat and broom away last Friday night."

Ben jabbed Ellen in the ribs. "What did I tell you?"

"Sh-sh!" Ellen said.

The woman was still talking. "I could do without that stupid broom. It never flew very well. My ankles were banged every time I went over a fence. But, oh, dear! It was a *lovely* hat." Two tears trickled down her pointed nose.

"What's your name?" Ellen asked. "You know ours."

"Gertrude," the woman said. "I've never liked it. Some people call me Gert. But I don't really like that either."

Ellen thought for a minute. "Would

you like it if we called you *Trudy*?" she asked.

The woman looked at Ellen. Suddenly her face cracked into a smile. "Why didn't anybody ever think of that before?" She gave three little jumps in the air. "Trudy, Trudy, what a lovely name!"

The candle was flickering. Ellen saw something on the ground right beside the candle. It was the earthstar! Ellen picked it up. A second later the candle sputtered and went out.

"I wish I had my flashlight," Ellen said.

She felt something heavy in the side pocket of her jeans. Ellen pulled out her little red flashlight. "I must have put it in my pocket after I finished looking for the frog last night," Ellen told herself.

She clicked on the flashlight.

"Lend that to me for a minute, Ellen," Trudy said.

Trudy shone the flashlight all over the cave. She bent over and poked her sharp nose into every crack in the rocks. "Oh, dear! Oh, dear! Whatever did I do with it? Next thing I'll be losing my head!"

"Is this what you're looking for?" Ellen held up the earthstar. "You were jumping around so much I was afraid you'd step on it."

"Yes, yes. That's my darling." Trudy gave Ellen her flashlight and took the little brown star. She held it on the palm of her hand. "Now, don't go running away again," she said to the mushroom. "I never seem to be able to keep track of you."

Ben poked Ellen. "I told you she took it last night," he said in a whisper.

"What's it good for?" Ellen asked Trudy. "Why do you want it so much?"

"I don't know," Trudy said. "But I just love it. When I was a child my mother had one. She would never let me touch it. Mother said earthstars were dangerous." Trudy frowned. "Yesterday this one changed me into a frog."

Ellen looked at her. "Is that why we didn't see you on the cliff?"

"That was dangerous all right," Ben said. "If I hadn't taken you home with me, you might have been eaten by a bird." He scratched his head. "And of course you know our names. You spent all that time with us yesterday."

"And now we know why we couldn't find the frog last night," Ellen said. "How did you get changed back to yourself again, Trudy?"

"The earthstar did it." Trudy slipped the star into the pocket of her green sweater. "I wish we could be friends," she said to Ellen and Ben. "I get lonesome all by myself here in the country."

"Where do you come from?" Ellen asked her.

"Brooklyn," Trudy said. "But the Head Witch there expelled me from the coven."

"Why?" Ben wanted to know.

For a minute Trudy didn't answer. She looked at the ground. "Lately I forget things," she said in a sad voice. "And my magic never did work well. Some of the other witches aren't very good either. But the Head Witch told me I was the worst she'd ever heard of. She said she wasn't going to let a good hat and broom go to waste any longer."

Bong! Bong! Bong!

Ellen ran down the passage to the mouth of the cave. She looked through the trees on the hill outside.

Ben and Trudy came after her.

"Ben, that's our motorboat out there! Mother and Daddy are looking for us. They brought along the gong." Ellen turned to Trudy. "Good-bye. We have to go now."

Trudy helped them over the ledge in front of the cave. Ben and Ellen climbed down the hill as fast as they could. They put the canoe into the water and paddled out into the middle of the lake.

10

Mr. Sanders was angry. "Don't ever go anywhere again without telling us. It's lucky our neighbor saw you two go out in the canoe or we wouldn't have known what happened to you."

Mrs. Sanders tied one end of a rope to the back of the motorboat. The other end was tied to the canoe. "I'm glad you had the sense to take the life jackets," she said.

Ellen sat down on the back seat of the boat. "I'm sorry you and Daddy were worried, Mother."

"We didn't want to wake you, Mom," Ben said. "You always like to sleep late when we're in the country."

The motorboat rumbled down the lake, towing the canoe behind it. The motor made too much noise for anyone to talk. Ellen liked the canoe because it was quiet. But the motorboat was much faster. Very soon they reached their dock.

Ben and Ellen jumped out and tied up the boat. Mr. Sanders put the canoe back on the sawhorses.

They all went up the hill to the cottage for breakfast. Mr. Sanders mixed up a batch of pancakes. Mrs. Sanders fried bacon and made cocoa.

Both Ellen and Ben were very hungry. Halfway through her third pancake, Ellen put down her fork. "Ben, what do you suppose Trudy eats? I didn't see any food in that cave."

Ben thought a minute. "Toads, I guess."

Ellen couldn't eat any more of her pancake.

Ben finished his. Then he jumped up and ran to look out of the big picture window. "Those birds sure are busy."

Ellen left the table and came to see what was going on.

Two brown birds were flying back and forth to the nest on top of the pole. There was no mother bird sitting there now. But four little beaks were sticking up out of the nest. The eggs had hatched.

"I wonder how those frog's eggs are doing," Ben said.

Mr. and Mrs. Sanders came to the window. They watched the birds for a while. Then Mrs. Sanders said, "I'm going to Hawley for groceries. There's a bazaar and rummage sale today at the Methodist church. I'd like to go to it."

Last year Ellen had bought an old book about water babies for ten cents at a Hawley rummage sale. "Oh, Mother," she said, "may I go with you?"

"Why don't you both run along right now?" Mr. Sanders said. "I don't much care for rummage sales. Ben and I can wash the dishes and burn the trash while you're gone."

11

Ellen and her mother drove five miles to the little town of Hawley. They stopped at the News and Novelty Shop to buy a *New York Times.*

"Oh, Mother, aren't they pretty!" Ellen pointed to a pot of pink and white petunias in front of the store.

Mrs. Sanders smiled. "There are even more flowers on Main Avenue than last year. Look at the windowboxes on the bank."

The library was open. Mrs. Sanders took out a book. "Why don't you take one out too?" she asked Ellen.

"I'm going to buy a book at the rummage sale," Ellen said.

Next they went to the supermarket. Mrs. Sanders bought four big bags of groceries. Ellen helped her load them into the station wagon. Then they drove to the Methodist church.

Some people stood outside on the church steps and talked to each other.

Inside there were two rooms with tables of things for sale. Mrs. Sanders went to the table with the biggest crowd around it. She bought a loaf of homemade banana-nut bread and a jar of watermelon pickles.

Ellen started to walk toward the table where there were books for sale. On the way she passed a rack of old clothes. On top of the rack was a pointed hat with a wide brim. Ellen stopped to look at it.

The woman in charge of the old clothes smiled at her. "That's part of a costume I wore in a play," she said. "I made it myself." She put the hat on her head and made a fierce face. "How do I look?" The woman laughed. "That's the way I looked in the play."

Ellen touched the hat. It was made of shiny black oilcloth glued onto cardboard.

"It's very strong," the woman said. "I wore it for a rainhat once. If you want it, I'll sell it to you for a quarter."

Ellen felt the hat again. She only had a quarter. "I really want to buy a book," she said.

She went to look at the books. There was a dog-eared copy of *The Cuckoo Clock* on sale for a quarter. Ellen loved the pictures in it, but she had already read the book. There were some great paperbacks too that Ellen hadn't read. They only cost a nickel.

But Ellen kept thinking about the pointed hat.

At last she went back to the old clothes stand. She took out her quarter and handed it to the woman there.

"Please, may I have the witch's hat," Ellen said.

12

"I thought you were going to buy a book." Mrs. Sanders put the banana-nut bread and the watermelon pickles in the back of the station wagon.

"I changed my mind," Ellen said. "It's such a nice hat." Ellen sat on the front seat and held the hat on her lap. "The lady who sold it to me said she wore it in a play."

Mrs. Sanders took a good look at the hat. She started the car. "I think I saw that play last summer at the Ritz Theater here in Hawley."

When they got back to the cottage, the breakfast dishes were all washed and put away. Ben and Mr. Sanders were down at the lake. Mrs. Sanders went into the kitchen to unpack the groceries. Ellen took the pointed hat into her room and laid it on her bed. She changed into her bathing suit.

"Are you going swimming?" Ellen asked her mother.

"I'll go later," Mrs. Sanders said. "Don't wait for me. I want to get a casserole into the oven."

Ellen put on her rubber clogs and ran down the hill to the dock. Mr. Sanders was sitting in the boat, trying to finish the crossword puzzle in yesterday's newspaper. Ben was lying on his stomach across the front of the boat. He was looking down into the water. "There are a lot of minnows down there," he told Ellen.

Ellen looked at the shiny little fish darting among the rocks on the lake bottom. Then she kicked off her clogs and dived into the water. She started to swim to a dock that was anchored in the middle of the lake. Ben jumped in and swam after her.

The water was just cool enough to feel good. Ellen rolled over onto her back and looked up at the blue sky. Swimming always seemed like flying.

Ben caught up with her. "Race you to the ski dock," he said.

Ellen would rather have drifted along in the clear water. But she didn't want Ben to think he could swim faster than she could. She rolled back onto her stomach and swam toward the dock.

They reached the dock at the same time. Ben climbed up a wooden ladder and lay down in the warm sunshine on the dock. Ellen came up after him. She brushed her dripping hair out of her eyes.

"I bought a hat for Trudy." Ellen sat down beside Ben. "It looks just like a real witch's hat. Maybe it'll cheer her up."

Ben sat up. "Did you believe that crazy story she told us?"

"Of course," Ellen said. "She's much too nice to be any good as a witch."

"That's what she wants us to think," Ben said. "You can't trust witches."

"You don't have to come with me if you're afraid," Ellen said. "But I'm going to take the hat over to her after lunch."

"Who's afraid? I just said I didn't trust her." Ben grinned. "Anyway, we never really explored that cave."

"Maybe we ought to take Trudy some lunch," Ellen said. "Only I don't know what she eats."

"Why do you worry about her so much?" Ben asked. "She looks old enough to take care of herself. I was more worried about her when she was a frog."

"Ben, if Trudy knew how to take care of herself she never would have been turned into a frog," Ellen told him. "She said the earthstar did it to her. No wonder her mother wouldn't let her play with them."

Ben thought about this. "Maybe you're right." He stood up. "Now we'd better take care of ourselves and get out of the sun. Remember that awful sunburn I got last year?" Ben dived into the water. "Race you back to the boat, Ellen."

13

"I thought you two had enough canoeing this morning." Mrs. Sanders looked up from her library book. "Well, be sure you keep those life jackets on."

It was after lunch. Mr. and Mrs. Sanders were sitting in the motorboat which was tied to the dock. Mr. Sanders was working on the crossword puzzle in the morning newspaper.

Ellen and Ben were still in their bathing suits. Ellen was wearing the pointed hat. It had black shoelaces sewn to it. She tied them under her chin so the hat wouldn't fall off.

Ben and Ellen put the canoe into the water and paddled away down the lake. When they reached Shuman Point, they beached the canoe. They left their clogs and life jackets in it and started up the hill to the cave. Ellen carried her little red flashlight in her hand.

They crawled up onto the rocky ledge and walked into the cave. Ellen shone her flashlight on the rough rock walls.

The walls were carved all over. People had scratched their names into the rock. Someone had written *June loves Bruce* with yellow spray paint all down one side of the tunnel.

"I guess it's not such a secret cave after all," Ben said.

They walked to the room where they had found Trudy. Ellen shone the flashlight all around. The floor was littered with acorn shells, but Trudy was not there. And there was no sign of the earthstar.

"I told you we couldn't trust her," Ben said. "The minute we left her she cleared out. Witches don't want anybody to know where they live. She's gone to make trouble somewhere."

"She can't be far away," Ellen said. "She doesn't have a broom to fly on."

"That's her story," Ben said. "But maybe she hid her hat and broom before she went to sleep. How did she get here in the first place without a broom? We forgot to ask her that."

They went out of the cave and climbed to the very top of the hill.

"Trudy! Trudy!" Ellen called.

The only answer was an echo, "Trudy! Trudy!" from the huge rocks on the other side of the lake.

"Come on, Ellen," Ben said. "I wish we'd never met that witch. Let's go back to the pool on the cliff and look at the frog's eggs."

They climbed down the hill to where

they had left the canoe. Ellen kept the hat on her head while they were paddling home. She was afraid it would get wet if she put it in the canoe. And she wasn't sure how waterproof it was, even though the lady said she'd used it as a rainhat.

When they got back to the cottage, Ellen and Ben changed out of their bathing suits. Ellen took off the hat and left it on her bed. It wasn't comfortable to wear. The shoelaces cut into her chin. Ellen was sorry now that she hadn't bought a book.

Ben's sneakers were still soggy. He put them on anyway. "Clogs aren't the best things to wear in the woods," he said. He pulled on a bright blue T-shirt.

Mrs. Sanders had come up from the dock to get her sunglasses. "Where are you off to now?" she asked.

"We're going to look at the frog's eggs in the rock pool on the cliff." Ellen followed Ben out of the cottage and up the path to the dirt road.

They took the shortcut over the hill. It was hot and sticky in the woods now. Ellen heard a buzzing noise near her ear. She slapped at it. "We should have put on some of that stuff that keeps bugs away."

Going down the cliff, Ben stopped to pick raspberries. "These are better than the ones I found yesterday."

Ellen sat down to dump the sand and pebbles out of her sneakers. Then she followed the old truck trail around the hill. She jumped over the little stream and started up the slope again.

When she came to the little pool, she bent over to look at the frog's eggs. "They're gone, Ben!"

14

Ben kneeled on the rocks beside the water. He looked into the pool. "What are those little black beans?" Ben reached into the water and tried to grab one. It wiggled away. "Hey, Ellen, this bean has a tail! It's a tadpole."

Ellen got down on her knees too. She stared into the water. "There are a lot of tadpoles hiding between the stones at the bottom."

Ellen pointed to something floating on top of the pool. "Ben, isn't that the earthstar?"

"It sure looks like it," Ben said. "But what's that funny bug on it?"

Ellen squinted to see better in the bright sunlight. Now she saw a tiny woman in a green sweater and a long brown skirt. She was asleep on the white puff-ball in the center of the star.

"It's Trudy!" Ellen said.

The star had been flat on the water a moment ago. Now, so slowly they could hardly tell what was happening, the brown points were turning down. The star began to sink.

"She's going to drown," Ben said.

Ellen snatched up the earthstar. She held it on the palm of her hand. It stood on its points.

"Looks just like an octopus," Ben said.

"Trudy," Ellen said, "wake up!"

The tiny woman sat up and stretched. She looked up into Ellen's face and seemed to be talking.

"What's she saying?" Ben asked.

"I can't hear her." Ellen lifted the earthstar to her ear. Trudy stood on tiptoe and shouted. But all Ellen could hear was a buzzing like a mosquito.

"Oh, I wish we could talk to each other," Ellen said.

Then she heard Trudy say, "No need to shout." She sat down on the puff-ball and crossed her legs. "I'm glad you finally noticed me."

"What do you mean?" Ellen asked.

"I tried to talk to you when you were in the woods," Trudy told her. "But you slapped at me and nearly killed me."

"I'm sorry," Ellen said. "I thought you were a mosquito."

"Aren't you going to thank us, Trudy?" Ben said. "We just saved you from drowning."

Trudy peeked over the edge of the puff-ball at the points of the star. "Oh dear, I forgot that earthstars go wild

when they're wet. This one was all curled
up like a nice little basket when I landed
on the pool."

"You mean that thing *flies*?" Ben said.

"It did when it was dry," Trudy told
him.

Ellen held the star up to take a good
look at it. "Do earthstars always fly?"

"I suppose so," Trudy said. "They do
all sorts of magic. But this one only
works when it wants to. And I never
know what it's going to do next."

"How did you get to be so small?" Ben
asked.

"The earthstar did it," Trudy said.

"Will it make you your right size
again?" Ellen wanted to know.

"I hope so," Trudy said. "But for some
reason it doesn't seem to want to."

The mushroom was drying out in the
sun. The points of the star began to lie
flat on the palm of Ellen's hand.

Ben looked at it. "Hey, wouldn't it be

fun if it was big enough for us to fly on
it? Trudy, see if you can work some
magic."

Trudy stroked the puff-ball. "Earthstar," she said, "won't you please take
my friends for a ride?"

Nothing happened except that the
points dried out a bit more. They started
to curl.

"You see," Trudy said, "there's no
telling what it will do."

"Oh, I wish Ben and I could fly with
you, Trudy," Ellen said.

The earthstar flipped its points like the flaps of an airplane. It sailed off Ellen's hand and landed beside the pool. Then it seemed to get bigger and bigger. So did Trudy. In almost no time she looked as big as she ever had been.

Ben and Ellen were still on their knees watching the star. Now they saw that everything around them was different.

They were near a small clear lake that was rimmed all around by strange bare hills.

Ben jumped to his feet and went over to the lake. "Ellen, look at these funny fat sharks!"

Ellen stood up. She ran over to see. "They look like giant tadpoles," she said.

15

Suddenly they both knew what had happened. Ellen looked at Ben. "The earthstar and Trudy didn't get bigger."

"No," he said. "We got smaller." Ben thought for a minute. "How are we going to get big again, Ellen?"

Even Trudy didn't know how to make herself big. She wouldn't be able to help Ben and Ellen. Ellen was scared, but she didn't want Ben to know it.

Trudy was calling, "Come on. I thought you wanted to go for a ride."

"Now's our chance, Ben. This ought to be fun." Ellen ran over to the earthstar.

The points of the star were starting to curve up around the puff-ball. Ellen squeezed between two points and climbed up beside Trudy.

Ben was right behind her. Now that he was on the earthstar he was so excited he forgot everything else. "Show me how you make it fly, Trudy."

"Watch." Trudy took hold of the tip of one point. She pulled it toward her. At once the earthstar flew up into the air. When Trudy moved the point to the right, the earthstar turned right. She pushed it the other way. The star turned left. "See?" Trudy said.

Ben nodded. "How do you land it?" he asked.

"Simple." Trudy pushed the star point forward. The mushroom flew down. It landed at the foot of a raspberry bush.

Trudy looked up at the juicy red

berries. "That reminds me," she said. "I haven't had lunch."

"Do you eat *raspberries*?" Ben asked.

"Love them," Trudy said.

"What else do you eat?" Ellen wanted to know.

"I had some nice acorns this morning. But what I like best are mushrooms. And sometimes they're very hard to find." She rubbed her pointed chin. "Come to think of it, I was looking for a mushroom when I found the earthstar."

"Can you eat earthstars?" Ben asked.

"Yes, but it's a terrible waste." Trudy slipped off the puff-ball and wiggled between the points of the star. She jumped to the ground and started to climb the raspberry bush.

Ben watched her. "I guess you're right, Ellen," he whispered. "She sure doesn't know how to take care of herself. Look at her now."

The berries were a long way up.

Trudy's brown skirt kept catching on the branches. "Ouch!" she said.

"What's the matter?" Ellen asked.

"I'm stuck on a thorn." Trudy tried to free herself. "Oh dear!"

"Stay where you are." Ben pulled one of the points of the earthstar back. The star began to rise in the air. Ben steered it between the branches of the raspberry bush over to where Trudy was caught on the thorn.

Ellen reached out and pulled the sharp thorn out of the back of Trudy's long skirt.

"Get back on the earthstar, Trudy," Ben said. "We'll fly over to a berry."

"Now why didn't *I* think of that?" Trudy climbed back onto the puff-ball.

Ben flew the earthstar under a ripe raspberry. It was almost as big as the puff-ball. Ellen stood on tiptoe and reached up to break off a round shiny piece of the berry. It spurted juice.

Ellen's arms were splashed all the way to the elbow.

The bit of berry seemed as big as a basketball. Ellen handed it to Trudy. "Here you are."

Trudy ate as if she were starved. Her cheeks were stained red. And her fingers dripped juice.

"I thought witches only ate toads," Ben said.

"Not me," Trudy told him. "I'm a vegetarian."

"You mean you don't eat meat at all?" Ellen asked. "Is that why when you were a frog you wouldn't eat the meat loaf?"

"Yes." Trudy sucked the piece of berry. "Some people say that's what's the matter with my magic. But I can't help it. I like to play with toads and frogs, so of course I can't eat them." She smiled. "Anyway, if I hadn't been turned into a frog myself, I never would have met you two."

She looked at Ellen and Ben. "I never really had such good friends before. I was lonely after the Head Witch expelled me from the coven. But I don't mind it so much anymore. If the sun weren't so hot on my head, I might not even miss my hat."

16

Ellen remembered the hat. She was sorry now that she hadn't brought it with her. They could fly home and get it. But Ellen wanted the hat to be a surprise for Trudy.

"Trudy," Ellen said, "there are some baby birds in a nest on our porch. We can't see them without climbing up. And Mother says that would scare the parent birds. I don't think the birds would be scared of us if we're this small. And on the earthstar we could fly right up to the nest."

Ellen just wanted an excuse to fly back to the cottage so she could give Trudy the pointed hat. But Ben didn't know what she was up to. He had always wanted to look into the nest.

"That's a great idea, Ellen!" Ben said. "How about it, Trudy?"

Trudy wiped her mouth on her sleeve. She dried her hands on the hem of her long brown skirt. "Let's go."

Ben pulled back a point. The earthstar zoomed up into the air. Ben steered it higher and higher. They flew to the top of the hill and over the trees to the other side. Then they cut across the road to the cottage. Ben steered the earthstar onto the porch and over to the pole in the corner. The star hovered just below the ceiling.

Ben and Ellen looked into the phoebes' nest. They saw four naked baby birds. Their beaks were wide open. And they were chirping with hunger.

The mother bird flew to the nest. She didn't notice the earthstar. She stuffed an insect into the beak of the biggest baby bird and flew away.

The father bird flapped over and fed a second baby. Then he rushed off to catch another insect.

Back came the mother bird. She dropped a mosquito into the open beak of the third baby and flew away.

"The smallest bird hasn't had anything to eat yet," Ben said.

"It's his turn now," Ellen peeped between the curled-up points of the earthstar.

The father bird flew to the nest. The biggest baby bird was chirping loudly again. The father dropped a fly into his beak and turned to go.

Ben stood up and waved his arms. "Stupid!" he yelled. "You forgot to feed the little guy."

The father bird caught sight of Ben's bright blue T-shirt. He swooped down and pulled Ben off the earthstar.

"Put me down!" Ben screamed.

But the bird didn't seem to hear him. He seemed to think Ben was some sort of fly. He flew to the nest and dropped Ben into the open beak of the smallest bird.

17

"Help! Ellen, *do* something!" Ben braced his feet against one side of the bird's beak and pushed his head and shoulders against the other side. If he could keep the beak propped open, the bird might not be able to swallow.

Ellen didn't stop to think. She stood up and made a flying leap off the earthstar.

She landed on the bare neck of the little bird and started to slide down.

One tiny pin feather was just poking through the skin. Ellen grabbed hold of it. With her other hand she tickled the throat of the bird.

The little bird coughed. Ben came flying out of the beak like a rocket. He shot up into the air and then fell onto the twigs at the edge of the nest.

"Ow!" Ben howled. "This is just like landing on a woodpile."

Ellen let go of the pin feather. She slid down the neck of the baby bird and hid under its wing. She peeked out and saw the mother bird flying toward the nest.

"Ben," Ellen screamed, "take off that blue shirt."

Ben pulled off his T-shirt and rolled it into a little ball. He sat on it. Then he leaned as close to the twigs as he could and tried to look like part of the nest.

The mother bird came flapping over. She didn't notice either Ben or Ellen.

The smallest bird gave another cough. It cleared its throat. The mother bird shoved a fat mosquito into its open beak and flew away.

As soon as the mother bird had gone, Trudy drove the earthstar right up against the nest. "All aboard!" she yelled.

Ben and Ellen jumped onto the puffball. Trudy started to back up the earthstar.

"Wait a minute!" Ben reached between two points of the star and grabbed his blue shirt off the twigs.

Trudy guided the earthstar down to the floor of the porch. She landed in front of the screen door.

18

The points of the dry earthstar curled over the puff-ball. Ben, Ellen, and Trudy were hidden from the birds.

Ellen felt as if she were wound up tight like a spring. Little by little she began to unwind. She peeked out of a crack between star points. "There's something in the house I want to show Trudy," Ellen said. "But we have to get the door open first."

Ben looked at the screen door. "The three of us ought to be able to do it." He slipped out of a space between points of the earthstar. Trudy and Ellen came out after him.

Ben grabbed the bottom corner of the door. He yanked at it until Trudy could get her foot into the crack. She spread her arms and legs apart to make the crack as wide as she could.

First Ellen and then Ben wiggled through. Then Trudy stepped out of the crack and into the cottage. The screen door closed.

Ben put his shirt back on.

Ellen walked to her bedroom. Ben and Trudy followed her. It seemed a long way away. Ellen was glad she had left the door of her room open.

"You have to climb onto the bed to see the surprise I have for you," Ellen told Trudy.

The blanket hung down almost to the floor. Trudy grabbed hold of the edge and climbed up. She was a good climber when there weren't any thorns to catch on her skirt. When she reached the top she waved to Ellen and Ben.

Then for a while they couldn't see her. She was walking across the bed.

"How do you like the surprise?" Ellen called.

"Do you mean this volcano?" Trudy asked. "I'd like it better if it had a fire in it."

Ellen had forgotten how big the hat would look. Trudy couldn't even tell what it was. Ben started to say something. Ellen put her hand over his mouth.

"Don't you dare tell her it's a hat," she whispered. "It would make her feel sad because she can't wear it." She yelled up to Trudy. "You can come down now."

They walked back to the screen door.

"One, two, three, shove!" Trudy said.

They all pushed together. The screen door opened a crack. Ellen slipped through first.

The earthstar was right where they had left it on the floor of the porch.

Ellen heard the sound of heavy footsteps coming down the wooden runway to the porch. She looked up to see the landlord, Mr. Barnes. He was bringing the mail.

Ellen got down on her hands and knees and crawled behind the earthstar to hide. Mr. Barnes walked over to knock on the screen door. He didn't see the earthstar.

The floor of the porch shook with each step the landlord took. He was coming closer and closer to Ellen. Suddenly she saw an enormous shoe coming down. Mr. Barnes was going to step on the earthstar — and on Ellen!

19

Ellen held tight to the edge of one of the points of the earthstar. The big shoe was almost on top of her now. Ellen shut her eyes. "Oh, I wish I was my right size," she sobbed.

"Oops!" Mr. Barnes said. "What in the world are you doing down there, Ellen?"

Ellen opened her eyes. The big shoe was gone. Mr. Barnes seemed to have shrunk.

He helped Ellen to her feet. "I don't know what can be the matter with me today. I didn't see you."

Ellen couldn't say a word. She looked around. Everything had changed. Suddenly Ellen knew what had happened. The earthstar had made her big again!

Mr. Barnes handed her the mail and walked back to his house.

Now Ellen saw that she was holding onto the earthstar by one of its points. She put it into her pocket and turned to look for Ben and Trudy. She couldn't see them anywhere.

Ellen opened the screen door.

"Don't step on us!" she heard Ben say. Ellen looked down. Trudy and Ben were still in the doorway. They had been standing in the crack.

"You really do look like a bug in that shirt," Ellen said.

"Don't be funny," Ben said. "Why didn't you change all three of us back to our regular size?"

"Yes, you'd better change Ben and me right away before anything happens to us," Trudy said. "I see why Mother told me earthstars are dangerous."

Ellen went into the cottage. She held the door open for Ben and Trudy to come in too. She put the mail Mr. Barnes had given her on the big table. Then Ellen took the earthstar out of her pocket. She held it up. "Make Trudy and Ben the size they ought to be."

Nothing happened.

"Please," Ellen said. "Pretty please?" She waited a minute. "Pretty earthstar!"

Ben and Trudy stayed small.

"I told you that earthstar doesn't work magic unless it feels like it," Trudy said.

Ben scratched his head. "Maybe it would feel better if we wet it."

Ellen put the star on the table beside the mail. She walked into the kitchen and took a paper cup from the dispenser. "Warm water or cold?"

"Try lukewarm," Trudy said. "That's the safest."

The screen door opened. Mrs. Sanders came into the cottage. She saw Ellen in the kitchen, which was only separated from the living-dining room by a low wall with a shelf on top.

"Ellen!" Mrs. Sanders cried, "what have you done to your hands?" She ran over to her. "Oh dear, I don't have enough bandages. I'll have to tear up a sheet. And we'd better get you to the doctor in Hawley."

Ellen looked at her hands. They were still stained with raspberry juice. And her arms were red up to the elbow.

"It's all right, Mother. Ben and I found a raspberry bush on the cliff." Ellen started to wash in the kitchen sink. "This is just berry juice."

"How many berries did you pick to get like that?" Mrs. Sanders asked.

Ellen didn't answer. She knew her mother would never believe she'd only picked a piece of one berry.

Mrs. Sanders walked to the bathroom. She took a bottle of Green Soap out of the medicine cabinet. "Come in here. I'd better wash you with this."

Mr. Sanders stepped in from the porch. "Where's Ben? I want him to help me put the tarp on the boat." He looked around the cottage and saw the mail lying on the big table. Mr. Sanders walked over to it. "What's this?" He picked up the earthstar.

Mr. Sanders started to call, "Ben! Ben!" He frowned. "I wish for once I could find that boy when I want him."

An instant later he blinked and rubbed his eyes.

Ben was standing right beside him.

20

Ellen looked out of the bathroom door. She saw her father put the earthstar back on the table. Then Mr. Sanders and Ben went down to the dock to cover the boat for the night.

As soon as her mother had finished washing her, Ellen went to the big table and picked up the earthstar. She put it into her pocket and looked around for Trudy.

There was no sign of her in the living-dining room.

"Ellen," Mrs. Sanders called from the

kitchen, "please set the table for supper."

Ellen went into the kitchen to get the plates and silverware. She looked on all the shelves. Trudy was not there.

When supper was ready, Mrs. Sanders banged the gong to call Ben and Mr. Sanders.

All during the meal Ellen was wondering what had happened to Trudy. She remembered how big Mr. Barnes' shoe had seemed. Ellen looked at her sneakers and then at her father's shoes.

After supper she swept the floor. Ellen looked hard at all the sweepings. She was afraid of what she might find. But all she swept up were crumbs from the table and dirt tracked in from outdoors.

"Thank you, Ellen," her mother said. "It's nice of you to sweep the floor for me. Daddy and I are going out in the canoe now. There's going to be a full moon tonight."

Mr. and Mrs. Sanders went out of the cottage and walked down to the dock.

It was Ben's turn to wash the dishes. Ellen dried.

"Where's Trudy?" Ben asked. "I haven't seen her for ages."

"I don't know." Ellen put the silverware in the drawer. "I've been looking for her."

Ben wrung out the dishcloth and hung it over the faucet. "I saw a spiderweb under the sink in the bathroom. It would be just like Trudy to get caught in it." Ben went to see.

Ellen finished drying the dishes. She went into her bedroom. The pointed hat was still on the bed. A little green and brown thing was curled up next to it.

It was Trudy. She was fast asleep.

Ellen remembered the earthstar. She took it out of her pocket and looked at it. It was dry and curly. Maybe Trudy ought to fly back to her cave on it, Ellen thought. She'd be safer there. There was nobody in the cave to step on her.

Ellen picked up the hat and looked around for a place to put it. There wasn't room on top of the little dresser.

"I wish the hat wasn't so big," Ellen said.

Suddenly she heard Trudy's voice. She had opened her eyes and was sitting up on Ellen's bed. "Where's the volcano?" Trudy wailed. "I've been waiting and waiting for you to light it up. I want to see how it works."

Ellen looked at the hat. It was so small now that at first she thought it had disappeared.

Trudy caught sight of it. She clasped her hands together. "Oh, Ellen," she said, "what a beautiful hat! And just my size!"

21

Ben came into Ellen's room. "I thought I heard Trudy's voice." He stopped short and stared.

Ellen was holding Trudy on the palm of her hand. Trudy had the pointed hat on her head with the shoelaces tied under her chin.

Ellen carried her into the bathroom so she could see herself in the mirror.

Ben came after them. "Be careful not to drop her into the washbasin, Ellen. She might go down the drain."

Trudy looked into the mirror. She smoothed her scraggly gray hair and straightened her brown skirt. Then she smiled at herself. "How do I look?"

"Just like a real witch," Ben told her. "But why didn't you make yourself big instead of making the hat small?"

"I had nothing to do with it," Trudy said. "Ellen has the earthstar."

Ellen had put the earthstar back into the pocket of her jeans. She took it out. "It doesn't look at all like a star now," she said. "But it still works — when it wants to."

"Give it to me." Ben reached for the earthstar. Ellen handed it to him. Ben held it under the faucet in the washbasin and dripped water on it. Slowly the points of the star turned darker. They began to uncurl and stretch out flat around the white puff-ball.

"Don't get the earthstar too wet, Ben," Ellen said. "It'll be like an octopus. And Trudy will have trouble reaching the points when she wants to fly on it."

"I don't feel like flying right now," Trudy said. "I'm hungry."

"Oh, Trudy, I'm sorry." Ellen carried her out of the bathroom and put her on the big dining table. "I didn't save you anything from our supper. I knew you wouldn't want lamb chops."

Ben went into the kitchen. "Do you like cornflakes, Trudy?"

"I like corn," she said.

Ben climbed on a chair and took down the box of cornflakes from the shelf over the refrigerator. He put the box on the table beside Trudy. Then he went to get a bowl and a container of milk. He held up the earthstar. "I don't know whether to ask the star to make the bowl small or Trudy big."

Ellen opened the box and took out one cornflake. It was longer and wider than Trudy. Ellen broke off a piece and gave it to Trudy.

Trudy nibbled the bit of cornflake. "Delicious!"

"You ought to have some milk," Ellen said.

Ben put the earthstar on the table and went back into the kitchen. He looked at all the bottles and jars in the door of the refrigerator. The bottle of lemon juice had a yellow cap with a hole in it to shake out the juice. The hole was covered with a small green cap.

Ben unscrewed the cap. "Trudy ought to be able to drink out of this."

Ben rinsed the lemon juice off the cap and filled it with milk. Ellen cut up a raisin with her mother's kitchen scissors. They put the cup of milk and the raisin bits on a small plate along with the rest of the cornflake. Then Trudy climbed up on the plate and sat down to finish her supper.

22

Trudy crunched through several bits of cornflake. She chewed for a long time on one of the pieces of raisin. But there seemed almost as much of that left when she finished as when she began.

Trudy wouldn't take the hat off when she drank her milk. The green cap was too big for her to lift. Trudy put her chin in the milk and lapped it up the way a puppy would.

At last Trudy rubbed her stomach. "I'm full." She stood up and walked to the edge of the plate.

Ellen picked her up and put her down on the table beside the earthstar. It was all spread out now and looked like a perfect star.

"Let's see if you're still in the mood to fly," Trudy said to the mushroom. She climbed onto the puff-ball and pulled back one of the points. The earthstar sailed up into the air. Trudy circled the room three times and then landed again on the table.

"Are you going to fly back to your cave now?" Ellen asked.

Trudy looked at her. "Oh, Ellen, do I have to? It will be so lonely. And I don't have any more matches. Even if I did, I couldn't light them. The matches are longer than I am."

Ellen took a look at the plate with the bits of raisin and cornflake on it. "You don't eat very much. And you don't take up much room. It ought to be easy to find a place for you to sleep," she said. "But don't let my mother and father find out that you're here. It might upset them."

Ben went into his bedroom. "Ellen," he called, "bring Trudy in here."

Ellen carried Trudy into Ben's room. He was bending over his dresser. The top drawer was open. There was a small matchbox in it. Ben folded a piece of Kleenex and fitted it into the box. "How's that for a bed?"

Ellen put Trudy into the matchbox.

Trudy untied her hat and took it off. Then she lay down. "Lovely."

"Where's the cover to the matchbox, Ben?" Ellen asked. "I think we can use it for a table."

Ellen used the kitchen scissors to cut a little tablecloth out of white notepaper. The scissors made tiny scallops all along the edge.

Ben put the table into the drawer. And Ellen set all the food left from

Trudy's supper on the white paper table-cloth.

Then Ben took a green twist-tie out of a box of plastic bags. He bent the twist-tie to make a little chair. It was rather tippy, so Ben used Scotch Tape to stick the chair to the bottom of the drawer. Trudy tried it. "Perfect!"

Ellen filled the top from a bottle of Seven-Up with warm water. She put it into the drawer and floated a scrap of

soap on the water. "I thought you might like a bath, Trudy. You're sort of sticky."

Trudy rubbed her chin. "I'll try anything once," she said. "It might be fun."

"Now you're all set," Ben told her.

"Oh, Ben," Ellen said, "I just remembered that Mother straightens your drawers. She leaves mine alone. She says I'm old enough to keep my own things neat."

Ben scowled. "You just want Trudy to sleep in *your* room, Ellen. It's not fair. It was my idea to make a bedroom in a drawer."

"But, Ben," Ellen said, "Trudy would smother if Mother dropped a pile of socks on her."

In the end Ben agreed to let Trudy live in Ellen's drawer. But he wouldn't help move the little furniture. Ellen had to do that herself.

23

Ellen heard the screen door bang. Her mother and father had come back into the cottage. She put the earthstar into her dresser drawer along with Trudy. Ellen left the drawer open a couple of inches so Trudy could have a little light and air.

"Better get to bed, children," Mrs. Sanders called. "You've had a busy day."

Ben was already in the shower. He went to bed without saying good night to Ellen. She knew he was still angry because Trudy was in her room instead of his.

Ellen undressed and rushed to get ready for bed. She was so tired she ached all over. The minute she lay down she fell asleep.

Sometime later in the night Ellen was wakened by moonlight shining through the window onto her pillow. She sat up in bed. Something whizzed past Ellen's ear.

It was Trudy. She was flying round and round the room on the earthstar.

When she saw that Ellen was awake, Trudy landed on her bed. She stepped off the earthstar. "Ellen," she wailed, "I feel awful."

"Was it something we gave you to eat, Trudy?" Ellen asked.

"No, no. Nothing like that. It's the moon," Trudy said. "It's full tonight. And at full moon time the witches have a meeting. I keep telling myself I don't mind missing it. But I do miss it. Oh, I do!" She covered her face with her hands and sobbed.

The door of the room creaked. Someone was coming in.

"Hide!" Ellen whispered.

Trudy ran under the edge of the blanket.

A moment later Ben stepped into the room. "Tell Trudy to cut out all the racket, Ellen," he said. "How can someone so tiny make so much noise? She woke me up. You're lucky it's my room and not Mom and Dad's that's next to yours. You know how mad Dad gets if you wake him." Ben noticed the earth-star on the bed. He picked it up. "Maybe we should send that witch back to her cave after all."

Trudy came out from under the blanket. Ben looked at her. He turned to Ellen. "What's the matter with her?"

"She wants to go to a witches' meeting," Ellen told him.

"You see," Ben whispered. "Once a witch, always a witch!"

Trudy's shoulders were shaking. She tried not to make any noise. But little sniffs and groans kept coming out of her.

"Trudy's really getting to be an awful bother to take care of," Ben said. "I just wish she knew how to take care of herself."

24

Trudy stopped crying. "Put the earthstar down, Ben," she ordered.

Ben and Ellen had never heard her
sound like that. It was a little scary.

Ben laid the earthstar on the bed beside Trudy. She held onto one of the
points and whispered something to the
star.

Wham!

Something knocked Ellen right out of
her bed onto the floor. She got to her
feet.

Ben grabbed her arm. "Look at the
witch!"

Ellen looked at the bed. A tall thin
woman in a pointed hat was standing

on it. She was holding the earthstar in her hand.

Ellen and Ben were really scared now.

The woman stepped down off the bed. "I'm sorry, Ellen," she said in a low voice. "I should have been more careful. Did you get hurt?"

"No," Ellen said. She was ashamed now that she had been afraid. Trudy was still herself, even though she was big again.

Trudy looked out of the window at the full moon. "It will be midnight soon. I don't have any time to lose. Didn't I see a broom in your kitchen, Ellen?"

"That's the old one that goes with the cottage," Ellen said. "It isn't much good. Mother usually brings one of ours from home."

"That one looked just right to me. May I borrow it?" Trudy asked.

"What do you want it for?" Ben said.

"They won't let me into the witches'

meeting without a hat and broom."
Trudy patted the pointed hat. "This hat
will do nicely."

Ellen tiptoed to the kitchen. She
brought back the broom and gave it to
Trudy.

Trudy sat down on the broom. She
whispered to the earthstar. The broom
rose in the air. It floated over to the
door.

It looked like such fun that Ellen forgot that she had ever been afraid. "Oh,

Trudy," she begged, "take me with you."

"Only witches are allowed at these meetings," Trudy said. She rubbed her pointed chin. "Wait a minute. I have an idea." Trudy bent over the earthstar and said something so softly that Ellen couldn't hear what it was.

Ellen turned to Ben. He put his hand on her head and scratched her behind the ears.

"What are you doing, Ben?" Ellen asked.

"Sh-sh. Not so loud," Ben said. "You don't want Mom and Dad to come in here and see you like this."

Ellen lowered her voice. "What are you talking about?"

Ben rubbed her back. "She's purring now, Trudy. Do you think she's trying to say something?"

"Of course," Trudy said. "Jump on the broom, Ellen."

Ellen jumped way up in the air and

landed on the bristles of the broom. She didn't know how she did it.

"That looks like fun," Ben said. "Can I go to the meeting too, Trudy?"

"I wish you'd asked earlier. I'm in such a rush that I can't think what to change you into," Trudy said. "Would you like to be a frog?"

"No," Ben said. "I want to be a cat like Ellen."

"Better not," Trudy told him.

"Please, Trudy," Ben said.

"Oh, all right. I don't have time to argue. I just hope this isn't a mistake." Trudy whispered something to the earth-star.

A second later a striped orange cat jumped onto the bristles of the broom beside Ellen.

25

Ellen held tight to the bristles of the broom. It was flying high over the rolling, tree-covered mountains. The moon was so bright that Ellen could see every whisker on Ben's furry face. A cold wind swept them along. The two cats kept close together for warmth.

"I wonder where the witches have their meeting," Ellen said.

"We'll soon find out," Ben told her.

"I'm glad you can understand me now.

But then, cats always seem to understand each other." Ellen looked at her
paws. They were darker than Ben's.
"What do I look like?"

"Like a real witch's cat — black." Ben
curved his neck and looked at his tail.
"I wonder why the earthstar didn't make
me black."

"Maybe the earthstar only did what
Trudy asked it to," Ellen said. "She
seems to have found out how to make it
work."

"I notice she's keeping the secret to
herself," Ben said.

"Oh," Ellen said, "I forgot Mother
told us not to go anywhere without telling her. Ben, we shouldn't have come."

"I wish we hadn't," Ben whispered.
"You can't trust a witch. But it's too
late now."

They flew over a bunch of lights. Ben
and Ellen looked down. But Trudy just
stared straight ahead.

"That must be a town down there," Ellen said.

The broom flew faster. Ellen felt the wind whipping through her tail. Now there were more towns. Then, in the distance, they saw tall buildings. A moment later the broom was over a river. Ellen and Ben could see the moon reflected in the water.

Seconds afterward Ben looked down. "We're right over the city, Ellen."

They flew over another river and then over rows of houses. The air was warmer here. Ellen saw a tower with a lighted clock in it.

The broom was coming down now. It swung over a highway and dived down to land on top of a hill. There were trees all around.

"We're here." Trudy hopped off the broom and shook out her long skirt.

Ellen and Ben jumped off the bristles. Trudy tucked the broom under her arm.

Battered old-fashioned lampposts stood here and there along a walk. They didn't give much light.

Ellen leaped onto the back of a broken stone bench. She craned her neck to look around. "Ben, I'm sure we've been here before."

Ben jumped up beside her. "Listen!"

Ellen heard the wail of a siren on a police car. There was the sound of cars rushing along a road at the foot of the hill.

Ben flicked his ears. "We're on top of Lookout Mountain in Prospect Park."

"Trudy told us she came from Brooklyn," Ellen said.

Trudy was going down the walk. It curved around the top of the hill.

"Come on," Ben said. "We'd better stay close to her."

The two cats jumped down from the bench and raced after Trudy. She was walking very fast.

"Halt!" a raspy voice said. "Who goes there?"

Ellen could feel all her fur standing on end. She looked at Ben. His yellow eyes were gleaming like two lights in the darkness.

A shadowy figure stood in the middle of the walk in front of them.

It was a witch.

26

"Don't you know me, Matilda?" Trudy asked.

"Oh, it's you, Gertrude," the witch said. "I thought you were kicked out of the coven."

"All a mistake, Matilda," Trudy said. "I'm here to see the Head Witch."

Matilda looked at Ben and Ellen. "What's this? Cats? You never kept a cat before, Gertrude. That was always a black mark against you. Well, I see you have a hat and broom. Go ahead."

The witch stepped aside. Trudy walked past her. Ben and Ellen had to run to keep up with her.

The path went around a small field at the top of the hill. The weeds were too high for the two cats to see over. But they could hear the sound of voices. And there was a strange smell in the air.

Trudy left the path and started across the field. The smell became stronger. Ellen didn't like it. She and Ben followed Trudy through the weeds.

They came to a big iron pot in the middle of the field. A small hot fire burned under it. Clouds of yellow steam drifted up into the air from the pot. It was the steam that smelled so bad.

Trudy walked toward the fire. A group of witches stood around it. They all wore pointed hats and carried brooms.

Most of the witches had cats. A mangy black cat raced over to sniff Ben and Ellen. He hissed and showed his sharp fangs.

Ben hissed back. "I guess he knows we're not really cats," he whispered to Ellen.

The cat backed away.

"Ben," Ellen said, "the witches are throwing something into the fire."

"I wish they wouldn't," Ben said. "I think that's what's making that awful stink."

"What do you suppose they're burning?" Ellen asked.

Ben strained his eyes to see. "It could be toads — or frogs," he said. "Maybe that's why Trudy wanted to turn me into a frog, so she'd have something to throw in the fire."

"Don't talk like that, Ben," Ellen said.

Now they both heard a yowling singsong. One of the witches was chanting.

Ellen put her paws over her ears. "Oh, Ben, I wish we hadn't come."

The witch who was chanting was taller and stronger looking than all the others. She had bright orange hair and orange fingernails. And the broom she had tucked under her arm had orange bristles.

"She must be the Head Witch," Ellen said.

Clang! The orange-haired witch banged her broom handle against the rim of the pot.

"That broom must have a metal handle," Ben said. "It makes almost as much noise as our gong."

"Inspection time!" the Head Witch said in a loud voice.

One by one the witches stood in front of the Head Witch. She looked at their hats and their brooms. When she saw Trudy's scraggly broom, the Head Witch nodded. "Very good."

She took a look at the hat. "Much too new-looking," she said. "Better put a dent or two in it."

The Head Witch caught sight of Trudy's face under the hat. She frowned.

"What are *you* doing here?"

Trudy didn't answer.

The Head Witch saw Ben and Ellen hiding behind Trudy's long brown skirt. "I suppose you think your having cats will make me let you in," she jeered. "Stupid! You know the rule is one cat per witch."

The Head Witch leaned over and grabbed Ben. "I'll take charge of this one. He just matches my hair."

27

The Head Witch held Ben up by the nape of his neck. "Just what I always wanted," she cackled, "an orange cat."

Ellen looked at Trudy. Why didn't she do anything? Trudy was holding the earthstar in her hand. She could easily save Ben.

But Trudy didn't move.

A cold chill ran down Ellen's back. Ben had been right all along. You couldn't trust Trudy. She must have known just how much the Head Witch wanted an orange cat. That's why she turned Ben into one. She was planning to use Ben to buy her way back into the coven.

Ellen saw the Head Witch's long

orange nails digging into Ben's soft fur. He yowled and tried to bite the witch. But she held him high in the air. Ben couldn't do a thing.

But Ellen could.

She made a flying leap at the witch.

The Head Witch saw her coming. She reached out and grabbed Ellen by the neck. Now she was holding both cats in the air. The skin on Ellen's neck was pulled tight. She was choking.

Suddenly Ellen heard Trudy's voice. "Put down those cats!"

"Make me!" the Head Witch jeered.

The next moment Ellen fell to the ground. Ben was beside her. But where was the Head Witch? Ellen couldn't see her anywhere.

Something wiggled out from under Ben's paw. It was small and gray, with a long naked tail.

"Catch that mouse!" Trudy yelled.

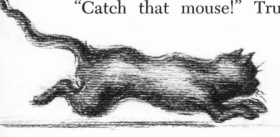

Ben jumped at it. But the mouse dodged him and ran around the iron pot. Ellen chased after it. Ben turned and went the other way around the pot. The mouse ran right into him.

Ben picked the mouse up by its tail and ran over to Trudy. He laid the mouse at her feet.

The mouse squeaked and jumped onto Trudy's broom. It climbed all the way to the top and sat there, shaking.

Ben got up onto the bristles of the broom. He stood on his hind legs to claw at the mouse. It clasped its little paws together and looked up into Trudy's face. Then it began to squeak.

Trudy held the earthstar to her mouth and whispered to it.

Now Ellen heard the harsh voice of the Head Witch. It was coming from the mouse.

28

"Gertrude," the mouse begged, "don't let those cats eat me!"

Ben jumped off the broom and sat down beside Ellen. "Ick," he said. "Who'd want to eat *her*? I just want to give the mean old thing a scare."

"Gertrude, you can join the coven. Only please change me back to myself," the mouse said.

Trudy just stared at her.

"You can be Head Witch, Gertrude," the mouse sobbed.

The other witches were silent. They stood around the fire and watched. The yellow steam drifted over them.

Trudy picked the mouse off the end of the broom. She held her by the nape of her neck just as the witch had held the cats.

"I don't want your silly Head Witch job," Trudy said. "And I wouldn't join your coven again for anything in the world. I see now that there are much better things to do with my time. I don't know why I came back to this smelly place at all. Just see that you leave my cats alone in the future."

"I promise, Gertrude," the mouse said.

Trudy whispered to the earthstar. At the same time she let go of the mouse.

Crash! The orange-haired witch fell

to the ground. Her hat rolled off her head.

Trudy sat down on her broom. Ben and Ellen jumped onto the bristles.

The Head Witch was crawling around on the ground, looking for her hat.

Trudy didn't bother to say good-bye to anybody. She pointed her broomstick at the sky. The broom sailed up into the air. Ben and Ellen looked down. For a moment or two they could still see the red glow of the fire. But they couldn't smell the yellow steam anymore.

They flew high over the city. The moon was going down now. And the sky was speckled with thousands of stars.

29

The broom flew so fast on the way home that everything under them seemed to be a blur. In almost no time they landed in front of the cottage. The two cats jumped off the bristles.

Trudy whispered to the earthstar. At once Ellen and Ben were back to being themselves. It felt funny to be wearing pajamas.

Trudy handed Ellen the broom. "It's the best one I ever had."

"I'm sorry you can't keep it, Trudy. But it belongs to the landlord." Ellen wondered what Mr. Barnes would say if he knew his broom could fly.

"I don't need it anymore," Trudy said. She held up the earthstar. "I'm going now. Thanks for all your help."

"You didn't really need any help," Ben said.

"Oh, yes, I did," Trudy told him. "You and Ellen helped me more than you know."

"Trudy," Ben asked, "are all earth-stars magic?"

"Every one," Trudy said. "But no two of them work the same way. That's what makes them so dangerous." She held the earthstar close to her mouth.

"Oh, Trudy," Ellen said, "will we ever see you again?"

Trudy smiled. "Of course you will." She whispered something to the earth-star. A moment later she was gone.

Ellen and Ben were quiet for a little while. Then Ellen said, "She never really was a witch, you know."

"What do you mean?" Ben asked.

Ellen stepped onto the runway leading to the porch. "Witches can't cry tears."

Ben thought about this.

"You don't have to be a witch to work magic with an earthstar," Ellen reminded him.

"That's right," Ben said. "And I'm pretty sure I know how that one works."

Ellen nodded. "I think I know too. And I'll bet we could figure out how to work another one."

Ben grinned. "Even if it's dangerous?"

"We'd better get back to bed before Mother and Daddy wake up," Ellen said. "Tomorrow we can look for an earthstar."

They tiptoed past the sleeping birds on the porch. Ellen quietly opened the screen door, and they went into the cottage.